For all my mates.

Once A Pawn, A Knight...

Written and illustrated by Cate Shainker

Once a Pawn, a Knight,

(And other pieces, too)
Found themselves together
In this story old and true...

"*MOVE!*" starts our story,
It came from the Knight
Who jumped up and down
On squares black and white.

"You frightened me, Knight!
And what did you say?
Why must I move?
Am I in your way?"

Pawn

Knight jumped a bit closer
And she pointed out
"We stand on a chessboard;
Look down if there's doubt!"

Knight told the Pawn
"It's your turn to move.
Our King needs protecting,
He's counting on you!"

Pawn said *"but I'm slow!*
I'm nothing like you!
I've seen how you JUMP!
Oh I wish I could, too!"

Knight liked that Pawn noticed,
And was eager to tell
How she jumps on the board

In the shape of an " L "

"Yes, I can jump forward, and I can jump back!
If I start on a **WHITE**, I end on a **BLACK**.
If I start on a **BLACK**, I end on a **WHITE**.
And now you know all about being a knight!"

"I jump 1, 2, 3
(So simple, you see?)
My moves are so rad!

Oh, what's making you sad?"

"All those jumps prove my point!
You make my head spin!
I'm slow as a turtle;
How could I help us win?"

"I can't move very far.
I can't move very fast.
Moving one at a time,
I'll always be last."

"NONSENSE DEAR PAWN!"
Knight said with a smile.
"One square at a time,
You have your own style..."

"...Diagonal to take,

Forward to move...

I know for a fact
The King would approve!"

"Well, I'll give it a try
For the King's sake."

...Forward to move...Diagonal to take...

The Pawn moved ahead
(But not very fast).
He didn't go far...

...But he *did* have a BLAST!

"YOU'RE DOING GREAT, PAWN!

...But this was no time for cheer.
The Pawn was in danger;
An opponent was near!

...and it was just

fine!

One square at a time
Was his key to success.
Pawn started seeing
He was GOOD at this chess!

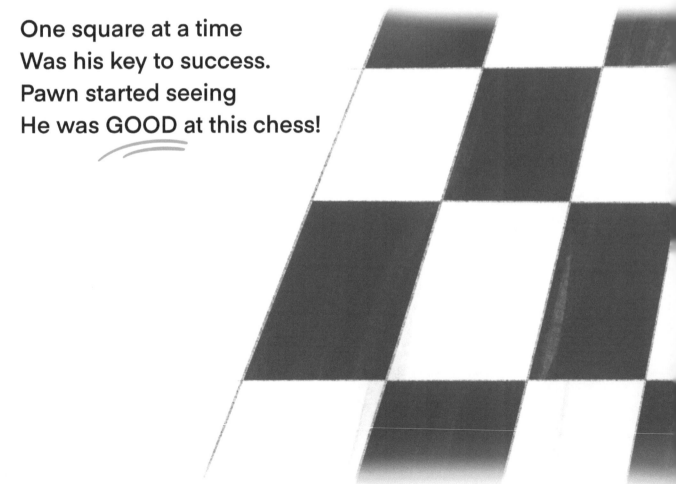

From across the chess board
Came a note from the King:

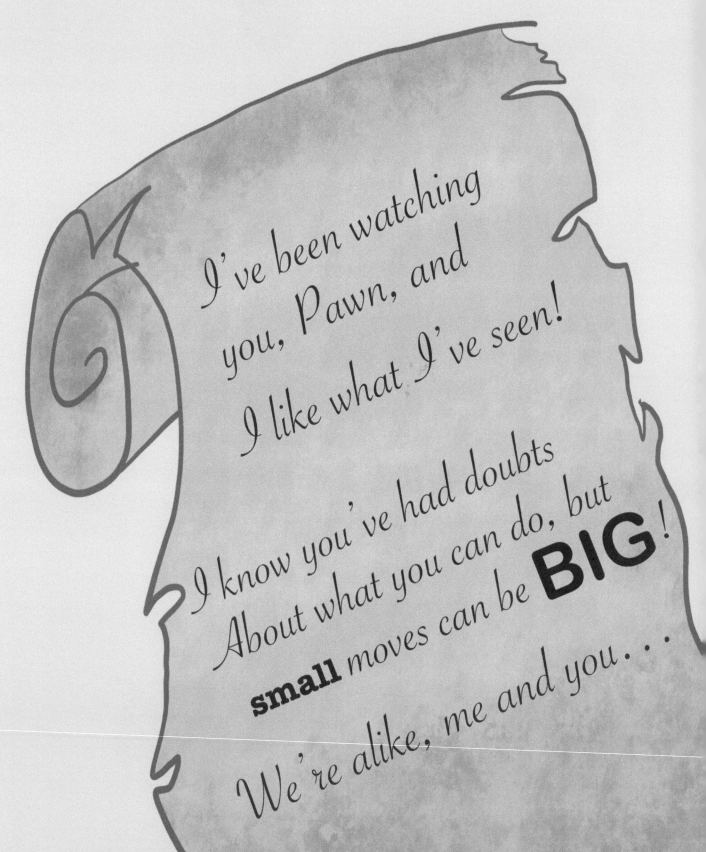

Knight asked of her friend,
"You see what I mean?
Your part is important,
And seen by the King!"

"I must be **straightforward;**

*You've helped me to see
I'm part of this team
By just being ME."*

You **JUMP**, others *glide*,

Some **z o o m**, and that's great!
I'm *slow* but important
And I found a ...

CAST OF CHARACTERS

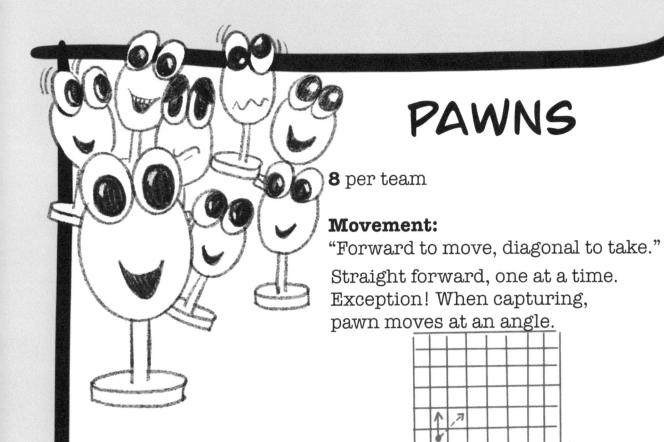

PAWNS

8 per team

Movement:

"Forward to move, diagonal to take."

Straight forward, one at a time.
Exception! When capturing,
pawn moves at an angle.

Special:
The pawn is the only piece to capture differently than it
moves. Plus, for its first move of the game, each pawn may
go forward **1 or 2** squares.

KNIGHTS

2 per team

Movement:
Shape of an "L" in any direction.

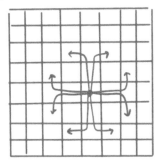

Special:
The knight is the only piece that can **jump over** other pieces.

KING

1 per team

Movement:
1 square at a time in any direction.

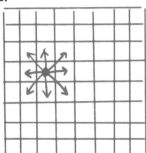

Special: Most important piece: capture your opponent's king to win. In **"check"** if threatened. **"Checkmate"** when threatened and escape not possible.

Stay tuned for more adventures on the chess board with Pawn and Knight!